Bigfoot and Joshua

Bigfoot

This Book Belongs To:

_____

Joshua

Writing this book has been a lot of fun. The talents of a gifted illustrator, Steve Ferchaud, made the task easier. Thank you, family and friends for your encouragement and suggestions. We dedicate this book to our four grandchildren: Megan, Preston, Erin, and Sterling, all of whom enjoy a good story. Bob and Peggy Bishop March 2008.

Text © 2008 Bob and Peggy Bishop (www.bigfootgifts.com)

Illustrations © 2008 Steve Ferchaud (www.steveferchaud.com)

© 2008 John Hinde USA (www.johnhindeusa.com)

Book layout and design by Ana R. Gonzalez

Art Direction by James C. Stevens

Joshua, his sister Emily, and his Mom and Dad were going on a camping trip to the mountains. They took food, tents and sleeping bags with them.

1

After a long ride in the car, Joshua and his family arrived at their campsite.

That night Joshua told his family that Bigfoot lived in the nearby forest. Emily laughed and said there is no such thing as Bigfoot. Joshua knew she was wrong and he was going to find Bigfoot.

3

Joshua and his family always had fun on their camping trips. They did things they could not do at home.

Joshua knew Bigfoot was in the forest and he wanted to find him.

5

He decided to go into the forest to find Bigfoot. Joshua did not tell anyone where he was going. He wanted everyone to be surprised when he found Bigfoot.

Later, it started to rain and Joshua was getting cold. He did not know that trees could grow this big. How was he ever going to find Bigfoot?

7

As soon as Mom and Dad realized Joshua was gone, they went to look for him. They asked the Forest Ranger to help.

8

Emily told the Ranger that she believed her brother went to look for Bigfoot. Emily asked the Ranger about Bigfoot. He told her that a lot of people believed they had seen Bigfoot in the nearby forest. They said Bigfoot was very big, hairy and smelled badly.

9

The Forest Ranger asked lots of people to help look for Joshua, but they could not find him even after looking all day. Mom, Dad, and Emily were very worried.

A lot of rain was starting to fall. The Ranger told everyone to stop looking because it was too dangerous to search in the dark. He said the search would start again in the morning.

11

Joshua was very sorry that he had left his family to look for Bigfoot. He was scared. He was lost and didn't know how to find his way back to the campsite. Joshua could not see how close he was to the edge of a cliff. Suddenly, he slipped and fell.

He heard a noise and smelled something bad. Joshua knew that Bigfoot smelled badly and was sometimes called the Skunk Ape.

13

All of a sudden a big hairy foot was in front of his face. He knew right away that the foot belonged to Bigfoot. Then Bigfoot's toes began to wiggle and Joshua got an idea.

14

Joshua used Bigfoot's foot like the saddle on a horse, wrapped his arms around Bigfoot's hairy leg and held on.

15

Joshua was suddenly face-to-face with Bigfoot. He was not afraid because he knew Bigfoot was his friend.

16

Joshua felt Bigfoot's strong hands under his arms. After a very short ride through the air, he was safe in Bigfoot's arms.

17

Bigfoot could see in the dark and knew his way through the forest. Because Bigfoot had such long legs, their walk to the campsite did not take long.

19

20 When they arrived at the campsite, everyone was sound asleep. Joshua pointed to his tent.

Joshua said, "I knew you were real. Thank you for saving me." Bigfoot zipped Joshua into the sleeping bag, patted his hand and left quietly after Joshua fell asleep.

21

22 In the morning, Joshua thought that maybe he had only dreamed about his friend Bigfoot. Then he noticed that his tent smelled as if a group of skunks had visited.

Joshua ran to his mom and dad's tent. He was worried that they would be very mad at him for going into the forest to look for Bigfoot.

23

Mom, Dad and Emily were very glad to see that Joshua was okay. He was sure they loved him more than ever. His Mom asked him, "Where have you been? You smell like a skunk!"

He told his family that he had gone looking for Bigfoot and that he had found him. Joshua told how Bigfoot lifted him from danger with his foot and carried him back to the campsite. Joshua could tell that no one believed him.

25

Just then his Dad saw some very large footprints in the soft muddy ground. Now everyone knew that Joshua was telling the truth about Bigfoot.

Mom told the Ranger how Bigfoot found her son and returned him to the campsite. She asked the Ranger to thank everyone who helped with the search and to tell them that Joshua was safe because of Bigfoot.

This was a camping trip that Joshua would always remember. He could not wait to tell all the kids at school about his new friend Bigfoot.

That night, Joshua dreamed that Bigfoot told his Bigfoot family about his new friend.

Frequently Asked Questions (FAQ) by young children

Q: Is this a true story?
A: No, but it could be if there was a real Joshua and a real Bigfoot.

Q: Are Bigfoots real?
A: We do not know for certain. Many people say they have seen them.

Q: Where have Bigfoots been seen?
A: More than two hundred people say they have seen Bigfoots in the California Redwoods and near Mount Saint Helens in Washington State. Willow Creek, California, is called the "Bigfoot Capital of the World" and has a large Bigfoot Museum.

Q: How big are Bigfoots supposed to be?
A: Between seven and eight feet tall, according to people who have seen them. If so, a Bigfoot's head could touch the ceiling in many homes.

Q: Where can I get Bigfoot children's t-shirts, children's Bigfoot puzzles and Bigfoot mementos for adults?
A: www.bigfootgifts.com